To whom inspired this work: My children

You're Bigfoot

By Ryan Montgomery

Illustrated by María Gómez S.

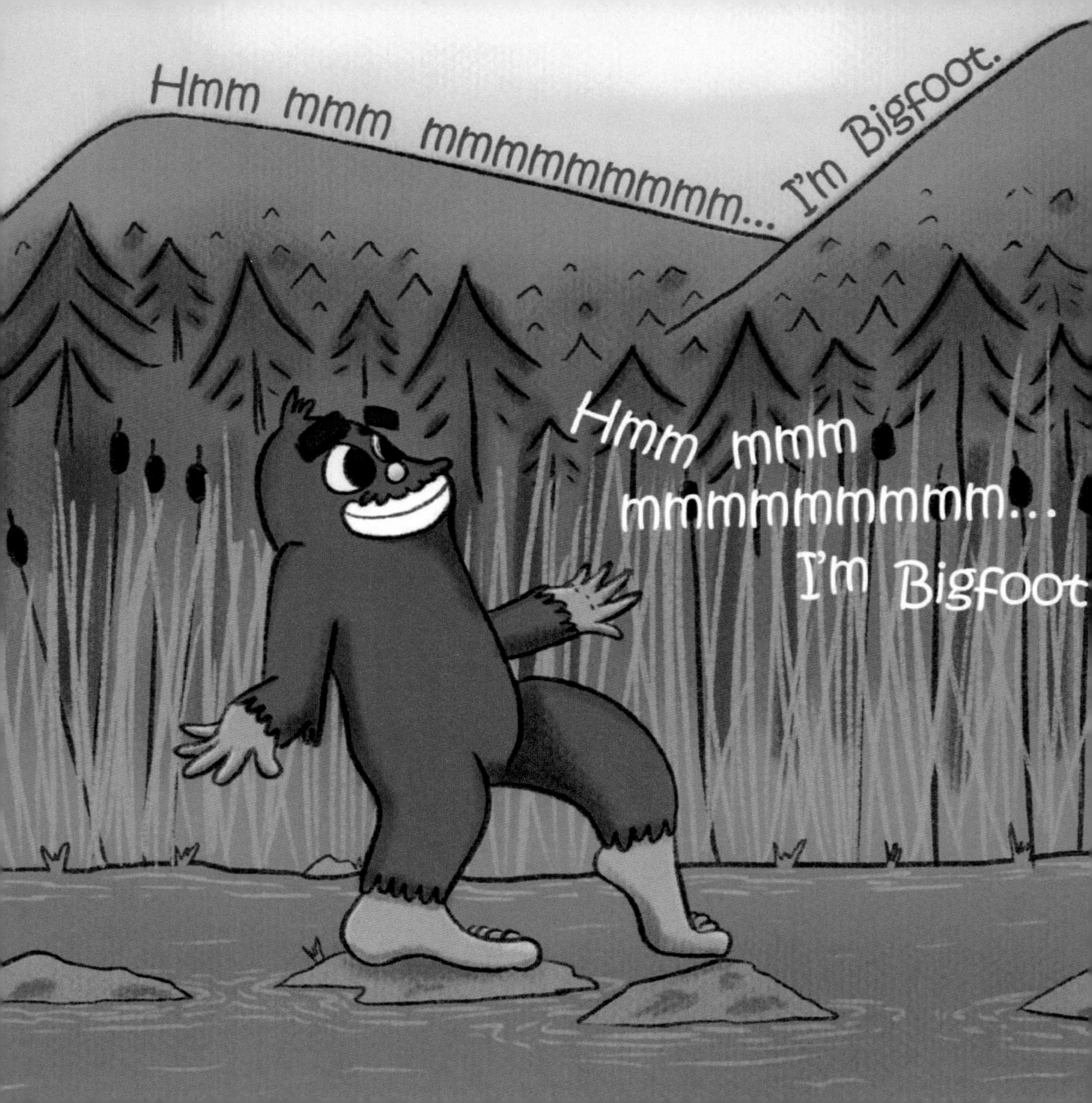

Hmm mmm mmmmmmmmm... I'm Bigfoot.

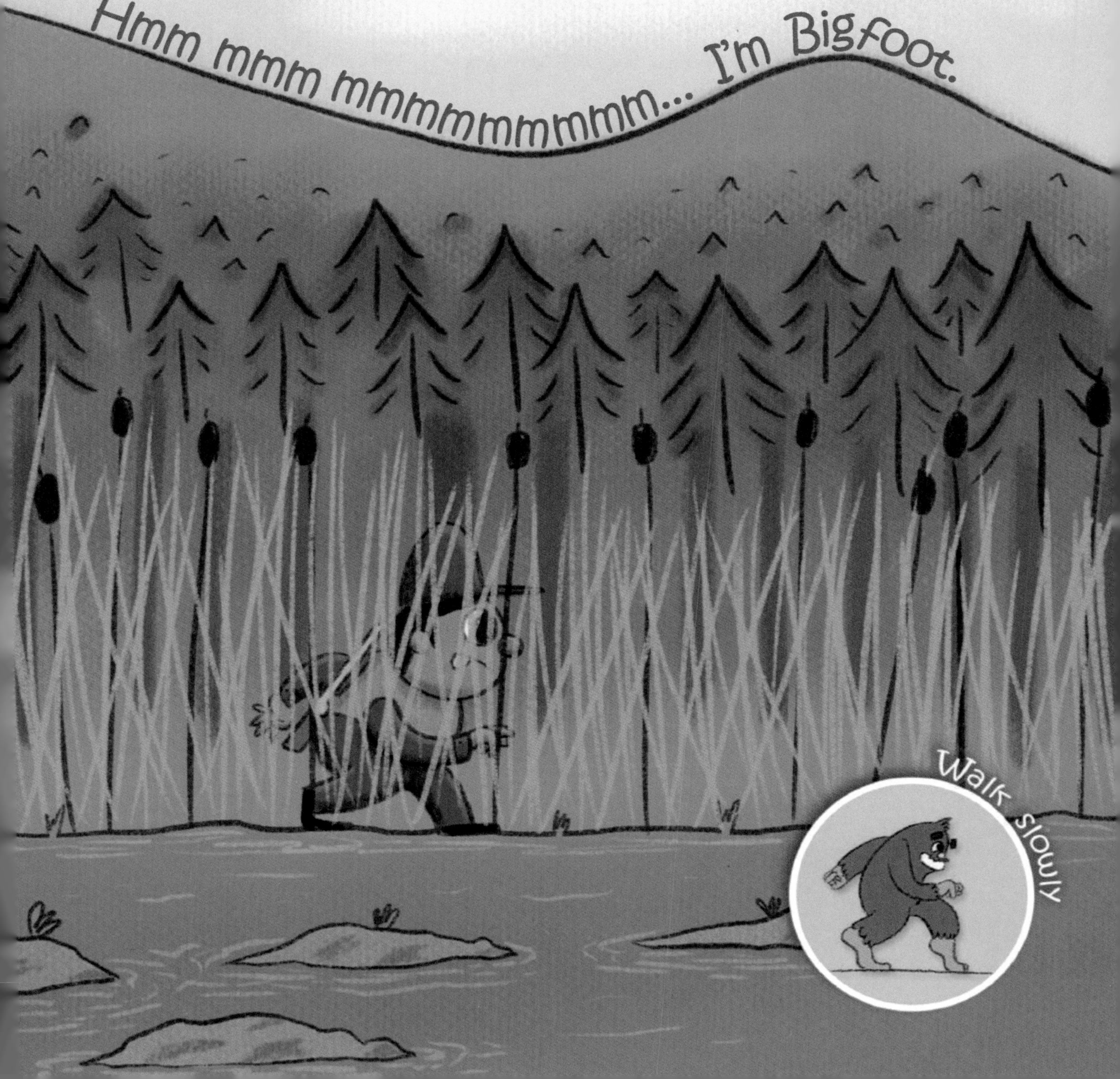

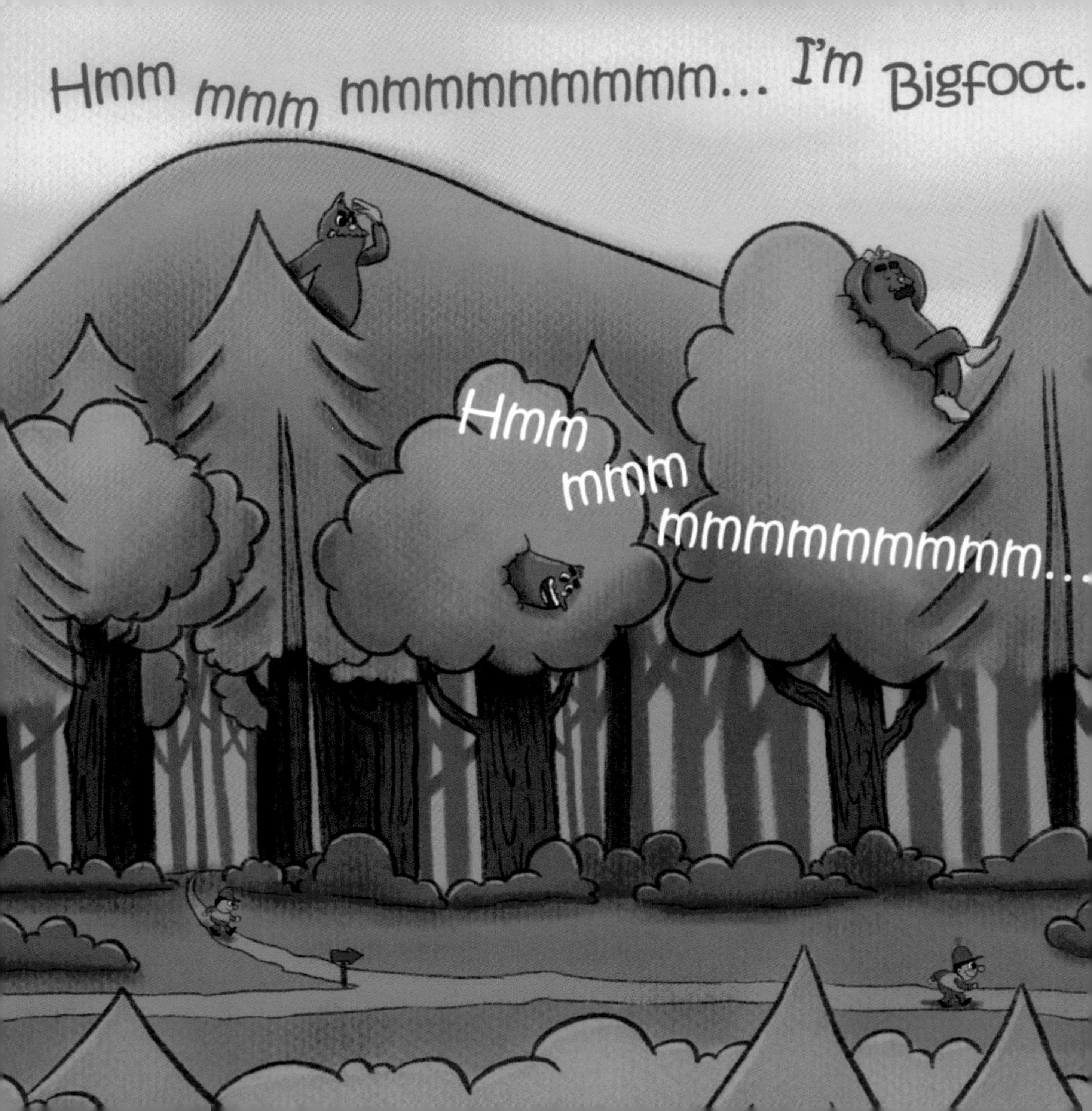
Hmm mmm mmmmmmmmm... I'm Bigfoot.
Hmm
mmm
mmmmmmmmm...

He doesn't see you...
Hmm mmm mmmmmmmmm... I'm Bigfoot.
Hmm mmm mmmmmmmmm... I'm Bigfoot.
Hmm mmm mmmmmmmmmmm... I'm Bigfoot.
Stick out your tongue

Hmm mmm mmmmmmm... It's bedtime.
Hmm mmm mmmmmmm... It's bedtime.
Hmm mmm mmmmmmm... It's bedtime.

Time to sleep

Move like Bigfoot!

Made in the USA
Monee, IL
07 December 2019